To Elise, Romy, Pierre,
Polly, and Orso

Copyright © 2023 by Kerascoët ✳ All rights reserved. Published in the United States by Random House Studio, an imprint of Random House Children's Books, a division of Penguin Random House LLC, New York ✳ Random House Studio with colophon is a registered trademark of Penguin Random House LLC.

Visit us on the Web! rhcbooks.com ✳ Educators and librarians, for a variety of teaching tools, visit us at RHTeachersLibrarians.com

Library of Congress Cataloging-in-Publication Data is available upon request.
ISBN 978-0-593-30767-0 (trade) — ISBN 978-0-593-30768-7 (lib. bdg.)
ISBN 978-0-593-30769-4 (ebook) ✳ The artists used ink and watercolor to create the illustrations for this book. ✳ The text of this book is hand-lettered. Interior design by Rachael Cole & Paula Baver ✳ MANUFACTURED IN CHINA
10 9 8 7 6 5 4 3 2 1 ✳ First Edition

Bear with me

Kerascoët

RANDOM HOUSE STUDIO · NEW YORK

Bear
with
me.

Bear. with. me.

Bear.   with.   me.

Bear
with
me.